Inspired by
A. A. Milne

Winnie-the-Pooh's Colors

With Decorations by
Ernest H. Shepard

Dutton Children's Books
New York

Published in the United States by
Dutton Children's Books,
a division of Penguin Books USA Inc.
375 Hudson Street
New York, New York 10014

Designed by Joseph Rutt
Printed in Mexico
ISBN 0-525-45428-4

Pooh's sweater
is red.

Piglet wears a red scarf.

Christopher Robin's front door is green.

Piglet wears a
green sweater.

Pooh floats under
a blue balloon.

The sky is blue.

Christopher Robin
wears a yellow hat.

The bee is black
and yellow.

Piglet picks purple
flowers.

Pooh has a purple
honey pot.

Tigger is orange.

Pooh and Piglet
walk toward an
orange sunset.

Rabbit is brown.

Eeyore's house is made of brown sticks.

Pooh is gold.

Pooh's honey
is gold.

Eeyore is gray.

The heffalump
is gray.

Pooh sits in a
pink chair.

The bathtub is pink.

Snow is white.

Christopher Robin
wears a white shirt.

The umbrella
is black.

Christopher Robin's boots are black.